Sparkly New Friends

UNICORN and YETI

Sparkly New Friends

written by
Heather Ayris Burnell

art by
Hazel Quintanilla

ACORN™
SCHOLASTIC

For Ellamae, who has always been an amazing friend — HAB

To my brother and sister, my Yeti and Unicorn from real life — HQ

Published in the UK by Scholastic Children's Books, 2020
Euston House, 24 Eversholt Street, London, NW1 1DB, UK

A division of Scholastic Limited.
London – New York – Toronto – Sydney – Auckland
Mexico City – New Delhi – Hong Kong
SCHOLASTIC and associated logos are trademarks and/or
registered trademarks of Scholastic Inc.
First published in the US by Scholastic Inc, 2019
Text © Heather Ayris Burnell, 2019
Illustrations © Hazel Quintanilla, 2019

The right of Heather Ayris Burnell and Hazel Quintanilla to be identified as the author and illustrator
of this work has been asserted by them under the Copyright, Designs and Patents Act 1988.

ISBN 978 0 702 30084 4

A CIP catalogue record for this book is available from the British Library.

Table of Contents

Something Sparkly

Unicorn saw something sparkly.

Wow!

Yeti saw something sparkly.

6

7

You live in the most sparkly place I have ever seen!

There are no sparkles where I live. It is white here.

There are **lots** of sparkles here!

No.
I will not leave.

We will leave!

Come on.
I will show you the sparkles.

Unicorn and Yeti flew up . . .

and up . . .

and down.

But mostly up.

The sun is very bright up here.

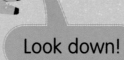

Look down!

An Amazing Friend

Unicorn, why do you have a horn on your head?

I do not know. I was just born this way.

24

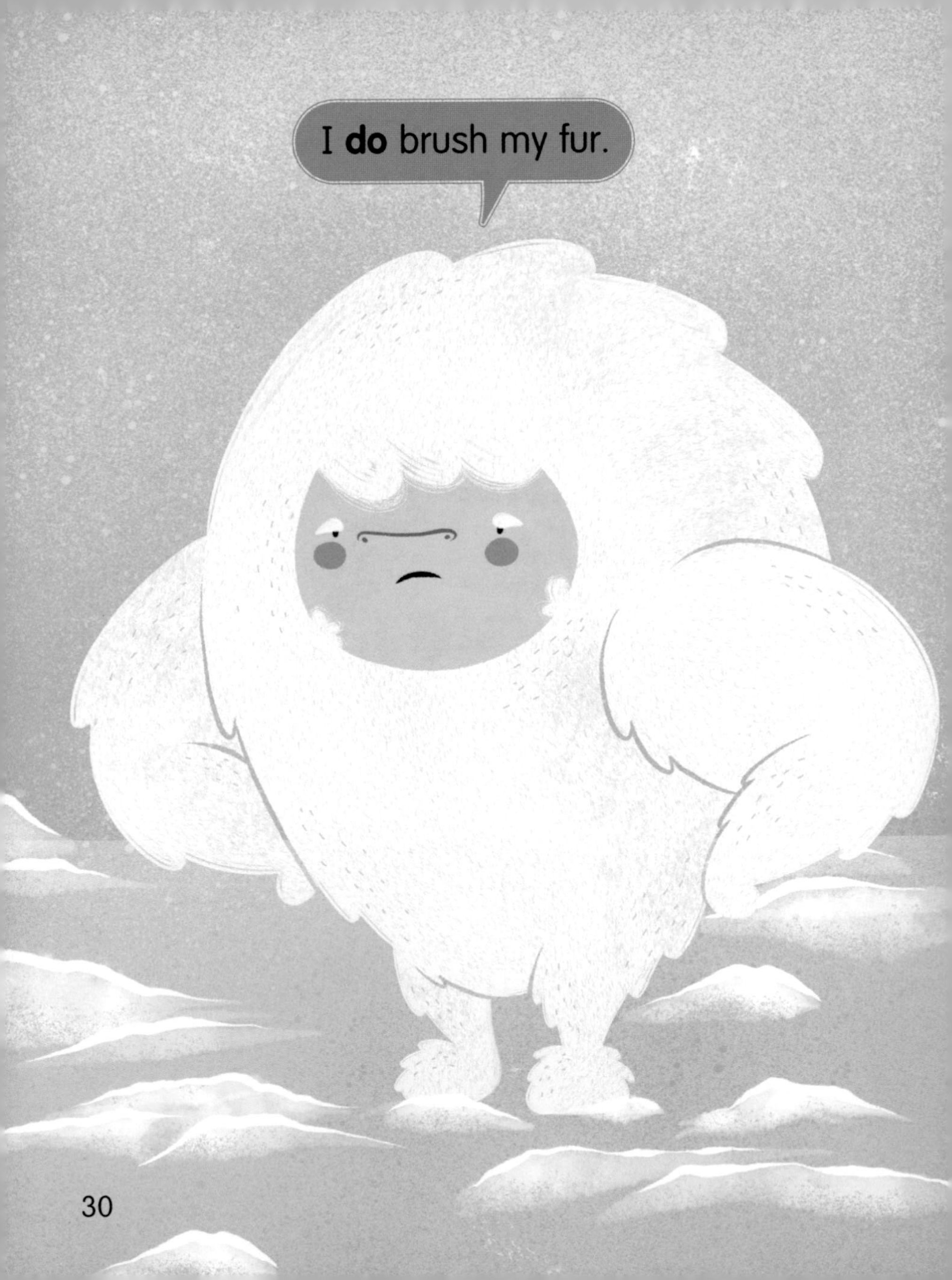
I **do** brush my fur.

You are an amazing friend.
I would like you even if you
could not do magic.

I know. You did not know I could
do magic until I just showed you.
And we were already friends.

Friends don't need magic
to like each other.

No, they
do not!

35

37

38

Snowball Fight

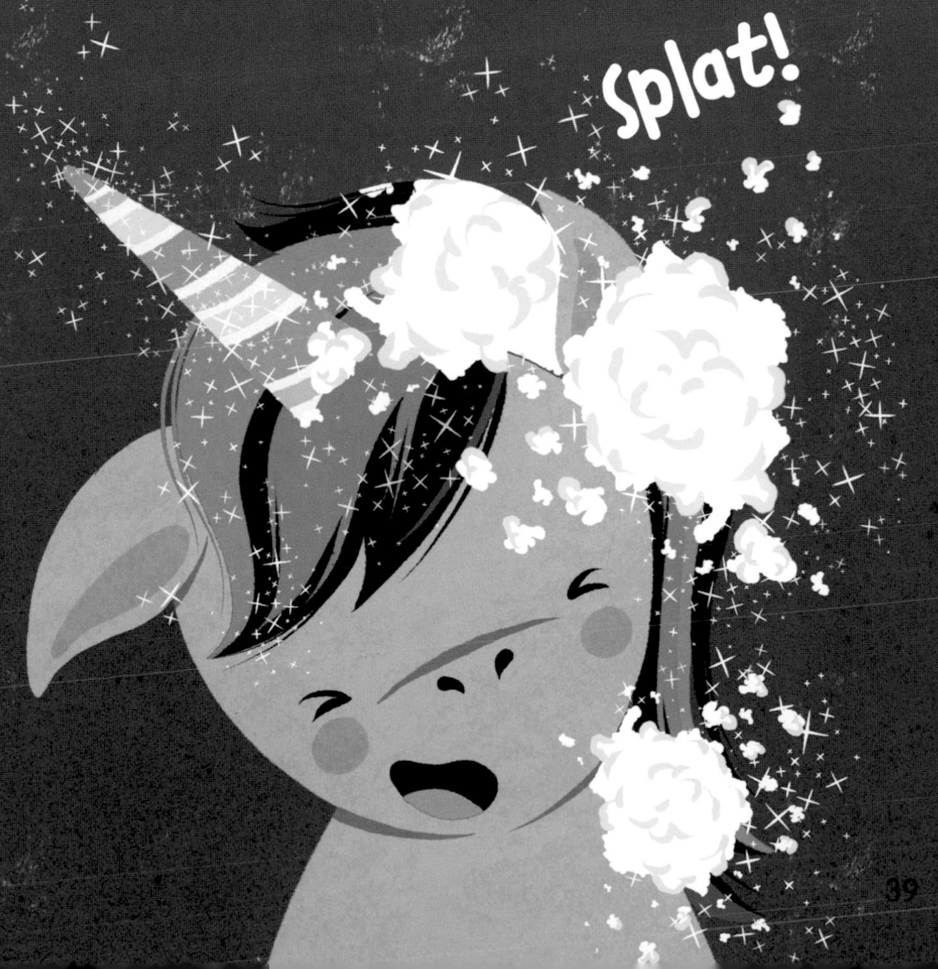

Did you **throw** that at me?
I thought we were friends.

It was just a snowball.

Throwing things at your friends
is not nice.

But throwing snowballs is fun.

First you make a big pile of snowballs.

Making snowballs is hard.

Next you build a fort to protect yourself.

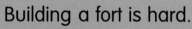

Building a fort is hard.

Isn't this fun?!

Splat!

I am wet.

You can do it!

I am cold.
I cannot feel my hooves.

Maybe throwing snowballs is not so easy when you have hooves instead of hands.

It is not easy.

I still think you can do it. Want to try again?

51

52

Let's go warm up. We can have some soup!

That's a great idea!

55

About the Creators

Heather Ayris Burnell lives in Washington state where she loves spending time in the sparkly snow. Sometimes she even has snowball fights with her friends! Heather is a librarian and the author of *Kick! Jump! Chop! The Adventures of the Ninjabread Man*. Unicorn and Yeti is her first early reader series.

Hazel Quintanilla lives in Guatemala. Hazel always knew she wanted to be an artist. When she was a kid, she carried a pencil and a notebook everywhere.

Hazel illustrates children's books, magazines, and games! And she has a secret: Unicorn and Yeti remind Hazel of her sister and brother. Her siblings are silly, funny, and quirky – just like Unicorn and Yeti!

YOU CAN DRAW UNICORN!

1. Draw a circle. Attach a larger semicircle below that. Then draw a smaller circle that overlaps the semicircle.

2. Add a snout and four legs.

3. Add one ear. Draw the face.

4. Add the other ear, a mane, and a tail. Then draw the horn!

5. Draw the details. Add stripes to the magic horn!

6. Colour in your drawing!

WHAT'S YOUR STORY?

Yeti wants to be fancy so Unicorn makes him a fancy hat.
What fancy thing would **you** make for Yeti?
What would Yeti do while wearing it?
Write and draw your story!

scholastic.com/acorn